ECHOES OF THE PAST

UNTOLD STORIES RESURFACED

WRITTEN BY PAULOMI BABRE

Dear Faint-Hearted Readers,

Take a deep breath. Remember, every story has its peaks and valleys. Embrace the journey, for it's often in the darkest moments that the light shines brightest. You're not alone; within these pages lie tales of resilience, hope, and the triumph of the human spirit. So, courage, dear reader. Keep turning the pages. The best chapters are yet to come.

With warmth and encouragement,

Paulomi Babre

(Child Budding Author of 10 Books)

Vote of Thanks

To come up to this level, there were a lot of people who helped me. Firstly, I would like to thank my mother, Mrs. Priya Babre for encouraging me to publish the book and to give such enthralling prompts. I would also like to thank my grandmother, Mrs. Usha Sivaraman, as she was the first step of my reading journey. I want to thank my father, Mr. Pankaj Babre, for his tremendous support. I would also like to show gratitude to my grandfather, Mr. Sivaraman for not allowing any obstacles to come in between. Lastly, I would like to thank my readers who have taken out time to read my book in this technology-lead world.

About the Author

I, Paulomi Babre am a 13-year-old living in Navi Mumbai. My hobbies include writing, swimming, baking and calligraphy. They also chose me as the finalist for creating and coding an app organized by CodeLQ. I have already published 10 books and more are there to come.

- ✓ The Village of Manapparai
- ✓ Super Seven Stories
- ✓ The Anime Express
- ✓ Venturous We
- ✓ Nurture + Culture= Future
- ✓ Life as it is
- ✓ Beyond the Box- Volume 3
- ✓ Fantabulous Five
- ✓ Story Arc
- ✓ 111 Stories on Love

I have taken part in and won many accolades in my journey of writing on various prestigious platforms nationwide. I have won several awards on the BTB platform (Beyond the Box) I have been nominated for many national Young Achiever awards. I also have my own website where I post my writings and other updates. I also own a business named Tassels where I make customized bookmarks, coasters, magnets, and wall hangings.

- My Email Id: unlockmemoriesbypaulomi@gmail.com

- Facebook: https://www.facebook.com/profile.php?id=61557295507680&mibextid=ZbWKwL
- Instagram: https://instagram.com/paulomibabre.8?utm_medium=copy_link
- Website: www.paulomibabre.com

Review by Debolina Coomar

A writer only begins a book, a reader finishes it.- Samuel Johnson.

As an avid reader and love of the genre, I simply could not get up without finishing the book. Gripping, power-packing, bone-chilling and enjoyable – each of these perfectly fit for this amazing anthology from our talented powerhouse, Paulomi. Each and every story adds a new flavour to the platter, making it an interesting read, for both kids and adults. I particularly loved the stories 'Sweet Revenge' and 'Who is Olivia' as it keeps the reader engaged till the end. I loved how a little Q&A was added towards the end to make the readers recapitulate the essence of each story. Paulomi has always been so good with words and expressions, both written and spoken. Having seen her grow with her literary passion, it has beautifully translated into her work. With every new book, she strives to try something new, and explore new ways to bring out her thoughts and ideas. And, it is wonderful to see a youngster diligently writing books, especially for kids.

Her love for the language, her articulation of ideas, and most importantly her dedication to at least write one book a year amidst her studies and exams are really commendable.

I wish her all the best for this new book, and many more to come. Never give up on your talent because always remember that if you WANT, you CAN CREATE WONDERS!

- Best Wishes,

Debolina Coomar

Author & Educator

Review by Anupama Dalmia

Echoes of the Past: Untold Stories Resurfaced is a collection of 8 blood-curdling, chilling, and thrilling short stories. Through these stories, Paulomi Babre takes the reader on a riveting journey of suspense, revenge, human emotions, and unanswered questions. At a young age, Paulomi truly displays a remarkable knack for storytelling that belies her years. Having been a mentor to her, I have been privy to her dedication to her craft and her natural gift to make words shine. But she takes it a notch up this time by exploring a range of dense themes. Each story, meticulously crafted, draws readers into its world, leaving them eagerly anticipating the next twist and turn.

"A Bloody Prom" sets the tone for the collection with its gripping plot and well-developed characters. Other stories that follow showcase the author's versatility as a writer, seamlessly transitioning between different flavours and tastes while maintaining a cohesive narrative thread of its genre. Her writing is marked by its clarity and maturity, demonstrating a keen understanding of human nature and relationships. Her descriptive prose vividly brings to life the settings and emotions, immersing readers in each story's eerie and curiosity-evoking atmosphere.

What sets this book apart is not just the engaging narratives but also the innovative addition of a Q&A section at the end. This unique feature allows readers to delve deeper into the characters and situations presented in the stories, offering added perspective and information, and enhancing the overall reading experience.

To sum it up, this anthology is sure to leave a lasting impression on readers of all ages. Paulomi Babre is undoubtedly a young author to watch out for, and I eagerly await her future literary endeavours.

Anupama Dalmia

Blogger| Karamveer Chakra Gold medallist| Author| Serial Entrepreneur| Social influencer| Founder and Chief Mentor of Beyond the Box| Founder and Choreographer of Rhythms & beats| Co-Founder & Website Designer at Tingle Your Taste buds.

Index

@@@@@@

A BLOODY Prom

"This emerald colour looks too good on your tanned skin!" exclaimed Chloe. Louise grinned and admired herself in the mirror. The gown was full-length. It had a halter neck and fragile bows. It looked luxurious and perfect for prom. Her bestie Chloe's baby pink dress was cutesier and stopped around the knee. They both couldn't control their excitement. It was their senior prom. They were getting ready at Louise's house. Their dates would come there. "Don't forget to take the boutonnieres from the refrigerator for Liam and Conrad. Come on girls, wear your heels and hurry up, they'll be here any minute. I want to take loads of pictures of you two," said Mrs Richard, Lousie's mom. Liam and Conrad had got corsages for them and after loads of pictures, they finally sped off to the prom. They took the standard prom couple pictures. Then, they joined their friends Martin and Clara.

The others didn't know this. Chloe and Louise were amateur detectives too. They often helped Chloe's dad, Mr. Dupont, a detective, solve some cases. Recently, they had been trying to solve a case about a dangerous gangster. Mr. Dupont feared that the gangster's men might come and harm the two girls. He had insisted that they wear panic bracelets. The bracelets would show their location on his phone. The girls had received a tip. It said someone might do something suspicious at the senior prom. So, they were alert at the slightest movement. The prom was at a club in their town. The club had 4 parts. It had the main dance floor and a smaller room for lounging. It also had the food and drinks area and a staff-only room by the back door. The dance floor was too crowded. The 6 of them went to the lounging area after grabbing a plate of wingdings and some fruit punch.

After snacking, they all started grooving and dancing. Louise and Chloe were having so much fun that they remained unaware of the dark plans unfolding. Chloe excused herself and went to use the washroom. Suddenly there was a short circuit and all the lights turned off. Everyone was screaming and frenzied. In the dark, Louise felt for Conrad's hand to avoid getting lost. The two of them tried to feel their way to the electricity mains. Louise turned her flashlight on and Conrad saw that somebody had snapped the wires. With much difficulty, Conrad rewired the mains and electricity came back.

Louise then suddenly remembered that Chloe was in the washroom. A strange feeling gripped her. She panicked," Conrad, Chloe was in the washroom. Suppose somebody has cut the wires. This means that somebody wants to cause a distraction. Let's find Chloe before it's too late!" Her date consoled her and they split up to find their missing friend. Louise went to the washroom. She checked every cubicle and even asked the janitor if a small brunette in a fluffy dress had come. But to no avail. Conrad checked with their group if Chloe had returned. They said no. So, he quickly explained the situation. Liam, Chloe's date had already started searching for her when the lights had gone and he hadn't yet found her. Louise tottered as fast as her heels allowed. She went up to the makeshift stage and asked the anchor to lend her the mike for a moment. Her delicate voice boomed across the club," Chloe Dupont, if you are there in the club please come to the stage. Please report to me, Conrad Robert, or Liam Blaise. if you see a short brunette in a pink dress. Thank you so much and please enjoy the party." She hopefully got down the stairs to see Chloe but she wasn't there.

After thanking the anchor profusely, she went to her friends. There, she saw Liam crying because he had searched the whole club but hadn't found her. He then left to search near the back of the club. On the spur of the moment, the lights went out again and this time the 4 of them held hands and stuck close to each other. It was 10 minutes before the lights came back. When they did, Clara squealed and pointed at the opposite wall.

YOU'RE NEXT, LOUISE RICHARDS!

Louise's face lost all its blood. Conrad protectively threw his arm around her. The writing looked gory, as if someone had written it with blood. Louise just hoped that the blood wasn't Chloe's. Louise gained composure and urged Conrad, "Can you please take me to Chloe's house? I'm sorry that your prom is getting ruined but please." Conrad nodded and said, "Anyways how am I going to have fun without you? So, the least I can do is drive you around." Soon they reached the Dupont residence and Louise raced to the front door while he parked the car. Kind Mrs Dupont opened the door and exclaimed, "Louise you?! Where's Chloe and what are you doing here? Weren't you both going to have a sleepover tonight?" "Aunty, I'll answer all your questions first can I please meet Mr Dupont? It is really urgent." Unfortunately,

Mr Dupont was out buying groceries at the supermarket. Conrad and Louise sat in the living room while Chloe's mom called him up to come as fast as possible.

By the time Louise calmed down and called her mom, Conrad had told Mrs. Dupont the whole incident. Louise told her mom that she would probably stay at Chloe's house. After hearing this Chloe's mom passed out. Louise who knew where Mrs Dupont kept her smelling salts, held the vial under the kind lady's nose and she soon woke up. Till then Adam, Chloe's dad had come and Conrad again narrated the story to him. Conrad was tired of telling the story. He excused himself and drove home. He had told the story three times. Louise and Adam went to his office in the basement.

Louise then recalled, "Uncle, you can check her location with the bracelet."" Yes dear, but it takes at least 3 hours to load. Till then, we must take action, right?" he replied. Through some advanced software, Adam retrieved the CCTV footage of the club. They saw Chloe going to the washroom. But, once it was dark, all they could see was that someone had put a handkerchief on her face and then had carried her away. Then, the footage just went blank. Louise then played the footage that showed the second power cut. They zoomed in on the wall. They saw the message and a youth wearing a blue suit writing it with a pail in his hand. Mr Dupont quickly took a sketch pad and drew a blonde youth donning a blue suit. He roughly estimated the height of the boy as 5'9" and that he was either a student or had sneaked in. After that, the screen showed static.

When it cleared, all they could see was couples dancing again. Louise was giving her announcement. "My child, I know you are really concerned for Chloe but you should get some sleep. Anyways till the location loads we can't do anything. Let's just hope for the best. Adam said, "I have also notified the police." "They said they will start their search tomorrow morning if we don't find her by then." Louise stifled a yawn. She went indignantly to Chloe's room, where Chloe always kept an extra pair of pyjamas. They had impromptu sleepovers many times. Sadness enveloped her as she slept on her missing friend's bed.

The next morning, without eating breakfast, she ran to Mr. Dupont's study. The location should've loaded by now. There she saw a rather puzzled Adam as the location showed the club! Without saying a single word, Louise ran up and phoned Conrad to meet her at the club. It was still early but as Conrad's dad was the mayor of the town the bouncer allowed them to enter and search the club. They stayed close. Nobody knew what lurked inside the club. This was especially true after the horrifying message for Louise. They searched the whole club. They decided to leave when Conrad remembered there was another room. "Louise, there is a room only for staff at the back end. We can check there too." The unlocked door creaked eerily. There was a strange rotten odour coming which was giving Louise a splitting headache. They switched on and Louise screamed. Chloe's mangled and badly disfigured body lay on the chair in front. The pink dress that she had spent all her savings on was now torn and covered with dried blood. The wall behind her had a message but this time it was not paint but blood which was used to write it.

HOPE THIS WILL TEACH YOU NOT TO MESS WITH ANTOINE.

"Who is Antoine?" asked Conrad after ushering her out in the sun as the room was too suffocating to stand anymore. Louise weakly replied, "H-H-He is the infamous g-g-gangster. You see, me and C-C-C-Chl-loe were helping Mr Dupont to find out more about him and arrest him. But his men cold-bloodily murdered her!" Soon the Duponts arrived and their devastation had no limits. A tearful Liam also joined the mourning. Louise thought," Enough is enough. Just because he's a gangster doesn't mean he can do whatever he wants." Louise's parents came to take their grief-ridden daughter home. On the other hand, the police were finally involved. Antoine wasn't easy. So, they appointed the best officials, Officer Erica and Officer Ethan, to solve the case.

Erica's wit and speed in solving cases made her well-known. She studied the case and said, "Hmm… I thought this was a simple murder. But, the message and senior prom is just too disturbing." Ethan was a lean youth, but he was also muscular. He reached his high position by solving a tricky case. It involved a lot of gunfire, smuggling, and fights. He solved it alone. He replied, "We should check the prom CCTV. We may have missed something." Erica had solved a case involving Antoine before. She said, "I suggest you stay in the police headquarters till we solve the case. Antoine's men will harass you till you drop the case." I'm going to research on Antoine now." Ethan said, "In the meanwhile I will go and talk to Louise Richards."

For the past 3 days, Louise has been cooped up inside due to the threat. She was happy to meet someone other than her parents. Ethan knew that it was hard for her and gently asked, "I hope you don't mind if I ask you a few questions. So can you just brief me a bit about what happened at the prom?" Louise who desperately wanted justice for her dead friend poured out the whole story. Ethan intently listened and made a few important notes too. Louise concluded, "They attacked her because we were both researching Antoine's crimes. We were about to find out about his drug dealings and other wrong-doings. But apart from us and Mr Dupont nobody knew about our research, so I don't know how they came to know." Ethan thanked her and was about to leave when they heard guns firing in the driveway. The young police officer grabbed Louise and ran down to the basement. Louise's parents also joined them there. Through the high window in the basement, they saw men in black masks shooting the house. After about 10 minutes, the men sat on their bikes and sped off. If he wasn't present, he knew he would have to rescue the three of them from being killed. So, he called the police to set up a room for the Richards to stay in until they solved the case. The family quickly packed essentials. They carefully stepped over the glass to go to the police car. It took them to the room.

Erica had researched a lot. She even sifted through old records. But, she couldn't find anything important about Antoine. She then went home where her grumpy mother made her go and collect the clothes from the launderers. While waiting for her clothes, a weary Erica sat around looking at the piles of clothes. Sparkly gowns, tartan plaid skirts, corduroy trousers, pinafores, suits and so much more. She looked away but something caught her eye. A blue suit! She quickly made sure no one was there and tugged at the suit which was right at the bottom of a huge pile. Yes, this was the same blue suit and it even had a red paint blob on the bottom of the lining! She took the suit to the manager, flashed her identity card and asked, "Look I'm Officer Erica. Quickly tell me whose suit is this?" The scared manager said, "Ma'am, I have only been here since yesterday. The workers told me that that pile of clothes has been here for the past 5 days." No one has made any records of the pile. The previous manager left 10 days ago. Until yesterday, all the clothes that had come had no records. But I can help you. I'll let you take the suit for investigation. If anyone asks, I'll tell them that I sent it for bleaching because it was a tough stain." Erica took her clothes and the suit after thanking the manager a lot. She saw that the blazer had a boutonniere so that person should be a student only. She phoned Ethan to meet at Louise's room in 5 minutes. Upon reaching there, Erica got to the point. "Louise dear, I don't want to pressure you too much. But, do you remember any student wearing this suit?"" Louise took the blazer and turned it around. Upon seeing the boutonniere she gasped, "This is Liam's blazer! This is the boutonniere Chloe bought for him. Now I remember that Liam was wearing a blue blazer." Ethan calmed her. He said, "Okay look. I need you to call Liam. Tell him to meet you and your friends somewhere. Erica and I will stand on the counter and pretend to order croissants. Once you guys have settled down, you hold the blazer up and confront him. From behind we shall pin him and done."

Louise hesitated for a moment but then thought of Chloe's body and newfound energy soared into her body. She first called her other friends. With the officers' permission, she confided in Conrad so he could back her up. She then lastly called Liam, "Hey Liam, the rest of us are meeting at the Little Tart bakery for some pain au chocolat. You are coming, right? Yeah- okay good. See you there." Erica and Ethan borrowed Mr and Mrs Richard's clothes and drove in their car while Louise rode her bike. Liam arrived last and quickly ordered a mocha latte and then settled down. Conrad patted Louise's hand reassuringly, and then Louise decided to go for it. She pretended to rummage in her bag for something and instead fished the jacket out. Liam's face turned red. He reached into his pocket for his gun. But, before he could act, Conrad, Ethan, and Erica pounced on him. They pinned him to the floor. The bakery's manager was already informed and thus he was least bothered. Martin and Clara who understood what was going on, ushered the other customers out. Louise used her heel to wedge the gun out of Liam's hand. Liam fought hard for 15 minutes. Then, he accepted defeat. Ethan and Conrad dragged him out to the police jeep.

After hearing Liam's confession, Ethan told Erica and the others, "What kids do for their dads these days?" He chuckled. The others slowly realized what he meant.

Corrupt blood on Vengeful hands

"My children, as you know these are my last words before I am reunited with your mother. The land adjoining our house is m-m-my only pr-o-o-perty. But I haven't made my will so you can split the house and land among yourselves. Good-d-d-bye," faltered Mr Rajaram as he took his last breath. His sons Krish and Abhi tried to hold a decent funeral but how much can two 21-year-olds do? Finally, after mourning for 13 days, they started to sort out all the debts and also split the property. "Phew! Baba has left a lot of debts. We have to pay a total of 12 lakhs! How much is there in his account?" said Krish who had just finished calculating all the borrowed money. His twin Abhi replied worriedly, "He only has 1.5 lakhs counting his account balance and spare cash he kept in the treasury. But there is some jewellery of Aai which we can sell or mortgage. We should get around 3 lakhs from that. But we still need around 8 lakhs to pay off the debts. I think we need to sell the land." Krish sadly nodded and said, "We should get a good buyer as the land is fertile and has so many flower beds planted on it. But we can't sell the house yet otherwise we shall be homeless. Until we get steady jobs, we can't afford to sell the house."

Krish stayed back to measure the land while Abhi went from house to house in their village for a buyer. Many of them were facing financial crises hence they wanted to sell off

27 – Paulomi Babre

their own house. Abhi decided to go to Mr Bakshi, the wealthiest man in the village for help. Mr Bakshi had a big heart and said, "Abhi, I will pay 9 lakhs for the land but on one condition the shrubs and flowers should be dug out and the land should be cleared of any plants. I plan on building a small school on that land so that the children don't have to travel 10 km every morning just to reach the school in the next town. So, you and your brother have to dig out everything. If you want, I will pay 10 lakhs but just clear the ground so that the architecture can start as soon as possible." Abhi thanked the kind man and promised to have the land ready within 15 days. Upon reaching home, he gave the good news to his brother who had been thinking of selling his books and cycle for money. The brothers took one last look at their majestic garden which bloomed bright bougainvillaea, sweet-smelling jasmine, honey-like tuberose, delicate plumerias and multi-coloured orchids before shoving their shovels in the mud. They had cleared the top layer of flowers within 2 days and Krish who had nimble fingers, made small bouquets of the good flowers and sold them around the village to earn a few extra pennies. The next day they made up their minds to rest and clean the house. While cleaning the living room, Krish stumbled upon a wooden box stashed under the cupboard. He opened it and it was filled with old yellow papers, he thought that they were just some odd papers about the house and stuffed the box inside again.

Abhi who was a good cook made them a delicious meal something that they hadn't eaten for a long time. They ate their chickpea curry, ladyfinger gravy, rice and flatbreads with the expression of starved men. The creator of the finger-licking meal said, "We got a good deal so the rest of the money that is left after paying off all the debts can be used to refurbish this old house." Krish said, "I have done architecture so at least I know the basics so I am planning to ask Bakshi if I can build the school." His twin brother nodded, "I think I am going to start catering for all the weddings and other functions that happen and I can also keep a truck for the tourists so that they can taste the local food." The two youthful brothers sat discussing their plans till dusk dawned.

The next day as they started digging the ground Abhi yelled, "There is something hard below the soil!" The brothers started digging there furiously thinking that like the tales even their father had left them treasure but to their horror, they unearthed a skeleton! Puzzled, they dug another path in the ground and to their dismay, there was another skeleton. "Why is our land lined with dead bodies?!" asked a baffled Krish. They quickly closed all the doors and placed a makeshift wooden fence around the land so that Mr Bakshi or some other villager wouldn't see the horrors unearthed from under the land. Abhi said," Krish come here! Look what I've found. Around 20 ID cards are there lying in the ground and all of them belong to government officials. Who murdered them? I hope it is not Baba." His brother worriedly sifted through the identity cards and without saying a word he went outside. He went to the local grocery shop where all the old men of the village always stood, gossiped and drank sodas for free. Krish also bought an icy, bubbly lemon soda and stood there. He then initiated a conversation with Bala Kaka, the biggest gossipmonger, "Kaka, was there any officer called Aditya Shah in our village?" Bala Kaka's ear perked up at the officer's name and replied, "Hey boy, I'm telling this to you only. He was a corrupt officer and because of him, many farmers have committed suicide. There were many more like him but then suddenly last to last year in June all of them passed away with one day gap between them. I think that some good angel came and made our already tough lives easier. But boy, remember

31 – Paulomi Babre

I didn't say anything and you didn't hear anything, okay? Now shoo!" Krish hastily ran from there satisfied with the little nugget of information.

He reached home and told Abhi all the news. He concluded, "So, whoever has murdered these people has done it with good intention as they all are unscrupulous. But before we give the ground to Bakshi, we must do something about this." Abhi determinedly said, "Within these 12 days we need to solve this mystery! But we should involve at least one policeman because this is a homicide. I think I know one guy who can help us. He is a retired policeman but he's wittier and fitter than the whole force combined. DGP Pillai stays on top of the hill and he will surely help us as Baba had once given his family assistance when they needed it." The twins went to his house and saw a lean man wearing a crisp white shirt and lungi. He was sipping on some coffee and twirling his moustache. After hearing their story, Pillai happily agreed to help them and immediately came down to their house. He mentioned, "If I am not wrong, this case is an unsolved one. For many years my colleagues and I had tried to solve it but we couldn't find the bodies only. But since you have found the bodies, I think I can unscramble the mystery within these 12 days." The brothers bountifully thanked him and the search then started. Pillai had also called two constables Rao and Nambiyar who were going to retire soon to help them. The constables adored DGP Pillai and came within 10 minutes of his call. The constables suggested that they search the whole land first and then proceed. All of them dug the land and checked every nook and cranny but nothing was found. DGP Pillai ordered, "Now we need to search the house. Krish and Abhi, you two search the bedroom, I will tackle the kitchen and you two take care of the hall. Off now!" After a lot of searching, Rao shouted, "Sir! There is a wooden box here with some confession letters. I think we have got a lead." Nambiyar added, "Sir, come fast! I'm sure this is the answer to the mystery!" Krish recognised the box as it was the same box he had hastily stuffed inside while cleaning the house. The senior officer quickly scanned through the letter and was shocked at the result. After reading the letter, he quietly asked the boys, "Your mother's name was Jaya, right?" The boys eagerly nodded, wanting to have a glance at the paper. "Well, she murdered these people, to say simply." Said the police officer. The boys and the constables gasped as Jaya was so sweet that she wouldn't even hurt a fly. Abhi flung himself on the retired gentleman and screamed, "You liar! How dare you say that my mother did something so sinful?" Krish who had been reading the letter, pulled his furious brother behind and said, "He's correct, Abhi. Read this and then if you are still not convinced then you can fight with him how much ever you want." His twin grabbed the letter and in a second all his anger vanished.

His mother had killed these government officials because they were shady and hollow-hearted. When her father was fatally sick and needed money, all the officials had told her and her mother to jump from counter to counter just to get his pension check.

Because of their corrupt nature, her father and millions around the country were suffering and died.

When she was diagnosed with cancer and had less time, she knew that she had to complete her mission. On every alternate day, she would give her husband nutmeg milk to put him to sleep and then she would go to that official's house, strangle the official quietly, stuff him in a sack and then bury that person in the land with a few seeds of flowers. All this was written by their mother in a letter so that after she passes away it could be used as evidence. Abhi remarked, "But she didn't die as per her cancer date. She died way before that. There must be some loophole." Nambiyar rummaged through the box and found another letter. He drawled," Sirrrr, there is one more letterrr!" All 5 of them peered into the letter and read. This letter was written by their father. The day when their mother murdered the 20th person, their father hadn't drunk his nutmeg milk. Their mother was covering the body with soil when she got caught. Rajaram was so astonished and angry that without thinking, he banged her head on the hand pump multiple times. She was a cancer patient and her body was already weak, so she died as soon as her cracked and weak head touched the pump the third time. Their father realised his folly after she passed away but it was too late. He covered the last body and, in the morning, when his children were awake, they were motherless.

Krish and Abhi were overcome with grief for their mother and hatred for their father. Pillai knew that they should be left alone and gestured the constables to follow him outside where they started piling the bones in a cloth and the ID cards were broken and thrown in the dumpster. The twins went outside and told the policemen, "You can take the letter and keep it as evidence and close the case. Anyway, since Constable Nambiyar and Rao are retiring, they will get better facilities because of this. We request only one thing, please close the case silently because we don't want to spoil the image of our lovely mother that is there in the villagers' minds."

Pillai patted the boys for their courage to give the letter.

Nambiyar and Rao went to the register of unsolved cases and proudly stamped SOLVED on the case. Pillai became a father figure for the two young boys. Mr Bakshi never came to know about the land and happily gave Krish the contract for building the school. Abhi became a renowned chef and for all occasions, his food was ordered. But the twins never forgot to donate large amounts to charity services for poor people so that in the future no other Jaya will have a compulsion to take lives to avenge her family...

Gory Greed

Ana Miller, a happy-go-lucky brunette was sitting in her office when her assistant came in running, "Ma'am, the police have asked for your assistance for some case. You are expected at the station in an hour." Ana sighed and thought, "Just when I thought of going on a vacation. I should've joined the police force instead of being a detective as anyways I am working on more cases with them than in my agency." She found that the case was about the murder of a 75-year-old woman, Mrs Brown who lived with her daughter's family. She was found dead at 8:03 in the morning by her daughter, Jules who had returned from her walk. At that time nobody was there at home. Jules had a husband, Jake and two kids, Mike and Melanie. The kids were staying at their aunt's place, Jake had been gone for a work trip for the past week and Jules was out walking. Ana was quite puzzled whether it was some other person apart from the family but as per her survey, 75% of the murders that occur at home are committed by a family member. The police officer in charge, Officer Smith informed that Jules and her kids were waiting in the lobby outside but Jake would arrive only after 2 days. Ana Miller went out to see a woman with mousy hair crying her heart out while her young toddlers kept asking, "Where is Grandma?" After offering some consolations Ana went back to her office so that she could work on the case in private.

What nobody knew was that Ana had the capability of reading the memories of the dead since childhood when she had started to miss her dead grandmother too much and started talking to her through memories. It drained all the energy of her body and for days she couldn't work again but it always helped her to solve her case more efficiently. She locked her cabin doors and quietly focused on Fanny Brown. As she started to forget about everything except Fanny her surroundings started swishing and everything became a blur. Everything was just a blur mess but Ana continued to focus on the old dead woman. But today despite all her efforts only a hand holding a blade came into her vision with a golden flash. She could hear wails and screams and then everything faded and Ana collapsed on her chair. It was too much of a strain and for 30 minutes she remained unconscious. As expected for the next two days she couldn't come to work and remained at home. She drank soup every day to recover. But the golden flash was just not going out of her mind. Something was odd but she couldn't put her finger on it. She was physically and mentally drained so she pushed all the thoughts away from her mind so that she could get some rest and start working again. Meanwhile Jake had landed from his business tour and Ana had got several calls from Officer Smith to come to the station and interrogate the family but she gave the excuse of having a high temperature because she couldn't share the real reason for societal reasons.

After a couple of days, Ana was fit enough to return to work. Smith ushered her to a room where the Brown family was seated for their cross-questioning. First, she called Jules inside the private room. She briskly asked, "So Jules, I'm going to ask you some basic questions and unless you've done something wrong, you don't need to be frightened. Okay so let's start. Can you give me a full description of your relationship with your mother? And please also tell me about your whereabouts on the day of the murder?" Jules who was intimidated by the detective's blunt nature meekly replied, "I have one sister and I am the older one. My mother and I were very close and were almost like best friends. When my dad passed away 3 years back, I decided to make my mother stay with me so that she doesn't feel lonely." Jules then swallowed some water as she felt tears forming in her eyes. She then continued, "On the day before her murder, it was her birthday. We celebrated it with pomp and had loads of fun. The next day I went for my daily morning jog with my neighbour Ellie and returned home at around 8. I rang the bell but mom didn't open the door. Luckily, we always keep a spare key under the mat and I entered the house to see my mother d-d-dead on the kitchen floor with b-b-lood sprouting from her skull. That's all." Ana made notes of the little chat and then asked her to send her husband in.

Jake was the elder son-in-law of the house. He was quite a jolly person and was a loving father. He entered the room and Ana asked him the same questions. He answered, "She was less of a mother-in-law and more of a mother to me. We both used to go out for ice lollies and I used to take her shopping too. She made amazing lemon grilled fish and chili rice and she made sure to make it for me whenever I craved it. In short, we had an amazing relationship. On the day of the homicide, as you might already know I was out on a business trip to Waterloo. I returned from my trip 2 days back. I have already submitted my hotel and flight details to Officer Smith so you can check my alibi from that." Ana thought that whatever he had spoken seemed too well-prepared and he was too confident and preppy for someone who's had a murder at their house. But since everything seemed fine on the outside, she refrained from cross-examining him more. Officer Smith had not permitted Ana to question the kids as they were only 3 and 5 years old. Ana was fine with that because toddlers couldn't possibly haul their plump grandmother on the floor and crack her skull unless they were ninjas or something in disguise.

Ana returned to her office and brooded for a long time. The gold flash kept coming to her mind but she just couldn't figure out what it was. She decided to do something she knew she would dread later. Ana decided to go back to the memory so that she could get a better view. She again focused on Fanny Brown and again the whizzing sensation occurred. This time she forced her mind to stop becoming dizzy and watch. As she was watching from Fanny's eyes, she saw a hand with a blade and the gold flash seemed to emit from the finger like a ring. She then lost her concentration and flopped on her chair. Again, for multiple days, she wasn't able to function but she had to haul herself up after 3 days as it was her childhood friend, Nancy's engagement. She looked quite attractive in her black sundress but she was exhausted. Nancy ran up to her and squealed, "Oh my gosh! I am so happy today. You know Josh (her fiancée) gave me a ring made of tungsten with a diamond because apparently tungsten is the strongest material for a ring and it won't get scratched!" Ana was genuinely happy for her friend and gave her a quick hug but then excused herself as she was too weary to be out for a long time and wanted to get under her covers quickly.

Before driving to her house, she took a turn and went to the Brown household. She rang the bell and little Melanie opened the door. Ana asked her, "Hello darling! Where are mommy and daddy?" "Waith, I'll call them othay?" lisped Melaine adorably. Jake and Jules came out together to the door and welcomed Ana into the house. Jules went to get some hot tea while Jake sat on the couch opposite Ana and asked, "I hope you don't mind, but what brings you here on a Sunday afternoon when 'normal people' spend time with their families?" The young detective sensed the dig and played along. She smiled and replied, "Well Mr Brown, you pay me for my job so I have to do my job properly right? By the way, it doesn't seem as though you are eager for the case to get solved. Why? Is there something I should know?" Jake was stumped for a moment at the detective's wit and they sat in silence till his wife joined them. Jules poured strong jasmine tea for

Ana for which the detective was grateful for as tea seemed to give her the energy to tackle the day. She sipped on her tea and then said, "I just wanted to look at the kitchen once since that was the crime scene. Also, can I have a word with your cute children just for a moment PRIVATELY? Jules and Jake glanced at each other nervously but then agreed as they didn't have any other choice because Ms Miller was glaring at them. They showed her the way to the children's room and wanted to enter when Ana stopped menacingly them, "Remember what I said? PRIVATELY. So, I request you both to head downstairs, sip on that lovely tea and relax." Ana entered the room and saw Melaine hugging her smaller brother as she had accidentally given him a paper cut. Melaine and Mike soon warmed up to Ana as the detective had treated his cut with gentleness. Mike liked the 'sweeth lady' as he called her because she removed his pain and Melaine adored her because she treated her darling brother. She then asked them softly, "Okay kids, now listen to me. I am going to ask you something but promise me you won't tell

Mama and Papa, okay? Did you both hear any fight before or after Grandma went away?" Mike glanced at his big sister who gave him a discreet nod and then he said, "Meli and I heardth that Gramma was giving her money to an umm…ch-ch-charioth." Melanie then primly said, "Noth charioth you twit, charithy. She was going to give her pennies to the charithy." She seemed quite pleased with herself for using such a big word like 'charity'. Mike then continued, "Later we heardth Papa complaining about the ch-charithy to his friend in a loud voice." Ana understood from the funny conversation that Jake clearly wasn't happy with the decision that Fanny had taken to give the money to charity. She kissed the children goodbye and walked out of the door with a mere nod at the couple.

After reaching home she took out her dusty but trusty notebook and her favourite gel pen. She then did something she used to do as an amateur. Ana wrote all her observations and suspects on the paper as it helped organize her mind. All her observations pointed to Jake. She then removed the mini camera that she had clipped to her clothing and swiped to the pictures she had clicked with it. Both Jake and Jules wore rings on their fingers but one of them had used it to crack Fanny's skull. Ana was pretty sure that it was Jake but to have solid proof she went to a jeweller nearby. She showed him both the pictures and told him to identify the metal it was made with. After much thought, he answered, "The woman's ring is most probably made out of pure gold. The gentleman's ring is made out of tungsten because it doesn't have a sSukhwinder scratch on it and exhibits all the properties of the material." Ana suddenly remembered Nancy's words about tungsten being the strongest material and her suspicion was confirmed.

She called Jake to her office and not the police station so that they could have a calm talk. He reached within 15 minutes and was rather annoyed to be called. He snapped, "Isn't it enough to meet us once a day? I am going to tell Smith to remove you from the case if you keep irritating us." Ana calmly smiled which infuriated Jake more. She then said, "Jake, I think it would have been better if you would have thrown that ring of yours. Sadly, it reeked of evilness and blood and now

I know that you murdered Fanny. Don't even try to cover up because I have solid proof." Jake looked at his ring for a moment and then said, "But Ms Miller this is Jules' ring. When I landed from my trip, she made me wear the ring because it was becoming tight for her and since my finger was thinner than hers, I agreed to wear it and gave her my ring which was loose for me. Ana does that mean..." Ana was shocked at the revelation and quickly went to another cubicle and logged on to the airport's CCTV footage and she saw that Jake **was** wearing the gold ring. She went back to her office where she saw Jake sobbing uncontrollably and she said, "Jake I know it's hard for you but we need to get hold of her. I need you to persuade her to sit with you in the living room and I shall take care of the rest."

The whole incident went as per plan and Jules was behind bars. She confessed that she had murdered her mother so that she could get all the wealth before she sanctioned a letter to the charity. Ana was quite proud of her skills at solving the case but all her pride washed away when baby Mike broke her heart by asking, "Where isth Mama, 'sweeth lady'?" Won't I see her again?"

---

51 – Paulomi Babre

DEPARTED AS 6; RETURNED AS 4

It had been a long time. There were a lot of fights unsolved, ties broken and promises forgotten. A reunion might join the bonds forever or sever them badly too. Cordelia Stirling wondered, "Will this reunion have a positive output or will some nasty things occur? I can think of a few people I don't want to meet but I guess I should go for the sake of old times." Cordelia Stirling was a 25-year-old blonde who worked as a home interior architect. She lived in New York alone and had kept in touch with only one of her school friends, Devina Hart.

All of them stayed in North America so they decided to meet at their previous hostel in Connecticut. Summer break was going on hence the management had allowed the alumni to stay at the hostel for 5 days. It was not only Cordelia who was sceptical about the get-together. All the other 5 of them were also doubtful about whether they should go or not. Cordelia's best friend Devina was in her own trance. She thought to herself as she packed her trendy suitcase, "I'm not going to act apologetic or grovel at anybody's foot. If they want to move on and talk, I'm game." Her clothes were bright and flowy and they showed that she didn't want to blend in and was fine standing out. She stayed in New Jersey and after the reunion, she was going to visit her great-aunt, Jemima who stayed in Connecticut.

The third puzzle piece of this group was Flynn Whitlock. He was an attorney in Philadelphia and was a jolly young man. He didn't have any enmity with the others but apparently, the other 5 had grudges with him. Flynn had always wanted to see his friends in the future to see whether everyone had turned out the way he had expected. Cormac Elrod was the fourth friend and he was a senior FBI agent. He solved cases through his agency as well as the cases that the police weren't able to solve or just didn't want to get involved in. He also stayed in New York and might fly together with Cordelia.

Belle Flair, an attractive young model was also coming for the reunion. She worked as a model and had won many pageants. She didn't have any problems with the boys as they hadn't gotten into a tiff but with the girls... To say lightly, they reacted like the same poles of a magnet (repulsion). The last friend was Declan Winslow, a Lieutenant Police officer. He was a muscular, quiet and straightforward guy. He didn't have any huge problem in meeting the others. Declan also had to visit the police headquarters in CT (Connecticut). He stayed in Massachusetts and since CT was just a 2-hour drive, he would drive.

Finally, the day of the reunion arrived. Cordelia and Cormac were slightly awkward at the beginning of the flight. But once they started reminiscing all the weirdness went away. They carefully avoided the fights and other mishaps and just focused on happy memories. In an hour they had reached Connecticut. Cordelia felt as though butterflies had built a nest in her stomach and were fluttering away to glory. She hoped that it would be easy to mSukhwinder with the others the way it was with Cormac. When they reached the hostel, all the memories just flooded into Cormac's head. Sneaking food from the cafeteria, dance-offs, last-minute projects, picnics and so much more. Devina had already reached and hugged Cordelia. Devina and Cormac had had their fair share of fights but they were just petty ones. They both were extremely intelligent and had a lot of competitiveness between them. But during times of need like when Devina's notes had been stolen, the latter had helped her.

The trio stood and merrily spoke until Belle Flair came. Cordelia and Devina immediately took their bags and moved farther behind. Cormac who knew about their quarrels wasn't surprised. Belle trotted over to them in her ridiculously high heels and handbag. She tittered and waved and looking pointedly at the girls she meanly said, "Wow, this is like a forced reunion, right?" Before any one of them could answer two cars entered the gate from the opposite directions and blew sand all over the others. Now it was time for Cormac to freeze as Declan had arrived. Once upon a time, he and Declan were best friends but their similar career choices and Flynn's arrival had turned their bromance bitter. Flynn gaily got out of his car, fist-bumped Cormac and waved at the girls. Declan got out of his car with deliberate slowness. He and Cormac exchanged forced smiles while Flynn high-fived him. Declan gave the girls quick grins.

The six of them stood silently for a long time until Flynn broke the silence by saying, "Guys, I don't think we are going to have the reunion at the entrance of the hostel. We need to head up and then we can sit and glare at each other." Everyone laughed at his raw honesty and headed up. Unfortunately, there were only two rooms—the girls in one and the boys in the other one. Devina groaned and indirectly said to Belle, "Ugh! I don't think it's legal for hyenas to sleep in rooms!" The latter scowled at her and Cordelia suddenly had a bad feeling about the next few days. The boys weren't having it any easier. Declan and Cormac had made it clear silently that they wouldn't sleep next to each other. So poor Flynn had to take the bed between the two grumpy guys. They all had decided that they would nap and relax for a while and meet at the cafeteria for dinner.

Cordelia who like Flynn had taken the middle bed said to Devina, "How long is she gonna shower for?! We need to go down in 30 minutes." Devina cackled and loudly said, "Maybe she wants to drown herself after looking into the mirror." Belle yelled from the bathroom, "I heard that!" "I meant for you too!" replied Ms Hart.   After 30 minutes of insults and chaos, the six were sitting for dinner. As it was a mere hostel cafeteria, all they had to eat was soggy hash browns, hamburgers and fried chicken that were moist. They were also served lukewarm Punch in goblets that clearly hadn't been cleaned in a long time. Their palates had a tough time adjusting to the food as they hadn't eaten such rancid food since their college days. "Eww... I just can't eat this. I'm going to get one of the microwaveable salads that I have packed. Thankfully I have got at least 15 of those, so I can live on them," said Belle and went away to the room to get her meal. Cormac did such a good imitation of hoity-toity Belle that Devina snorted loudly and spilt all her juice on Cordelia's white cashmere hoodie. "Seriously Devina! On my hoodie?! I am going to get cleaned. I'll be back in a moment," said an annoyed Cordelia. Devina also ran behind her to help. There was an edgy feel to the table as only the boys were left. Flynn who was sick of trying to start a conversation every time, sat sullenly. Declan suddenly found his disfigured hash browns fascinating and Cormac looked at the ceiling as though he had seen it for the first time. Cordelia and Devina returned shortly and continued with their meal. Declan then noticed, "Hey it's been more than 30 minutes since Belle went. Don't you guys think we should check on her?"Any which way they all were done with their 'amazing' meal so they agreed. The search party first went to the girls' dorm and when they entered, they saw her sleeping on the bed. Flynn rolled his eyes and said, "Seriously we got so panicked just to see her snoring?" Cordelia went over to the bed and then suddenly yelped. "Guys she had fits!" Cormac who was an FBI agent and had worked on the forensic team previously, slapped her face a few times and then checked the white foam on her mouth. He then gravely said, "She's dead... She was poisoned with a type of venom that is deadly just by touching." Immediately all the boys looked at the girls. Declan said, "Look, you both were the only ones who had left the table at the same time as Belle. Secondly, you both also came to the room so that Cordelia could get changed. So... it's obvious that we will suspect you two first." Devina and Cordelia were aghast at the statement. Cordelia angrily retorted, "A petty squabble during our college days isn't a motive to commit such a sin! How dare you accuse us? It could be you guys too as there are slow poisons too." Flynn remarked observantly like the lawyer he was, "You seem to know a lot about various poisons." Devina glowered at him and was about to say something when Cormac cut her off, "Guys, we can play the Blame Game afterwards. First don't you think we should do something about her body?" Declan roughly said, "Since **I'm** a police officer, I am going to go to the station nearby and see what can be done. Till then don't allow the hostel management to find out." Before leaving he mentioned, "Put some perfume in the room. After some time, the rotten decaying odour will waft out of the room."

The others sat in complete silence and just stared at Belle's once beautiful face now turning cold and blue. In a short time, Declan returned and said, "I've convinced them to let me lead the case. Since obviously the murderer isn't going to admit it, investigations will start by me. Cormac, I know we don't have a great history but since you are an FBI agent I will need your help. Flynn let me know what are the charges for such murder and also research on the murder. You two ladies, please sit in the room or go down to the garden. Everybody is forbidden to leave the grounds except me because I need to go to the station to give regular updates." The girls were very offended by the way they were treated but decided to sit in the garden and be out of their way. The boys were caught up in their search for clues and more. But they couldn't find anything. It was almost midnight and everybody decided to turn in for the night.

At around 1 at night, Flynn woke up to rustling in the room. He quietly switched on his lamp and saw Declan packing his bag. Declan hadn't noticed the light yet and was rummaging furiously for something. Flynn quietly asked, "Are you looking for this, Declan?" He held a small blackish-green vial in his hand. Declan whipped around, saw the bottle and gritted his teeth, "Ah you little imbecile! You found out. Alas! Now you shall die how that horrendous Belle died." He advanced towards Flynn who sat on the bed calmly when Cormac entered the room with a team of armed FBI agents. Cormac said, "I was always right to stop trusting you. Come on and wear these handcuffs like a good boy." Surprisingly, Declan didn't put up a fight. The girls also came in running.

Flynn then explained, "Tonight when we were searching, I had a bad headache and came back to the room for some aspirin. Although I didn't find the aspirin, I did find this vial falling out of your bag. Cormac instantly identified the poison and then it was easy. Now tell us your motive." Declan who was normally placid, banged his fist on the table and said, "She deserved to die after what she did. You see my sister; Diana was also a model. Belle knew that Diana was better than her and that she had no chance of winning. She staged a lot of incidents as though Diana was mentally unstable. Belle went to the extent of asking a friend of hers to give a fake medical report that Diana was mad, bipolar and dangerous to others. She was shipped off to a camp for mental people and now she isn't allowed to leave it. Staying with genuinely sick people, my sister is starting to get influenced. Belle ruined her life and career. Then why should she live happily?

 Declan was arrested and put on trial. Cordelia and Devina were out of suspicion. They had left as 6 people but returned 4 with one dead and one as good as dead. While submitting Declan's confession, Cormac and Flynn made sure to mention Belle's wrongdoings and Diana was immediately released from the camp. Upon hearing the news, Cormac mentioned, "Brother and sister relationships are like Tom and Jerry's. They infuriate and tease each other but without the other, they can't live."

Guiltless Death

"Hello, please help me!! He's going to kill me!!" screamed a distraught woman on the phone. Insp. Aman Malhotra frantically said, "Try to defend yourself by some means and buy time. We will reach there immediately!" Spontaneously he told his team to track the location of the call and with a few constables he got onto a jeep to the location. A man snatched the phone before the woman could reply, "Come and get me if you dare. By the time you reach here, I'll be long gone and she'll be dead." Usually, the location was just a 7-minute drive but out of all days there was heavy traffic at that very time. The location showed 5 minutes by car and 8 minutes by walking. Aman and a small team of constables got down and ran the rest of the distance, as by jeep it would take a lot of time. They reached just in time to see a masked man leave the house with a bloody knife. The inspector realised that it was too late to save the woman so might as well catch the murderer. The team surrounded him from all sides and by then the other constables also reached in their jeep. His eyes turned wide and woebegone. Mr Malhotra noticed it and was sure that there was some other reason and not his capture. While the constables handcuffed the murderer, the inspector went inside the house and saw a woman lying on the floor with her head hanging on just a bit of flesh. Fresh blood oozed out of her neck and when he turned the body around, he found that the knife had been inserted into the woman's back and resulted in a hole in her stomach. A few constables took the body to the nearest morgue to keep her till further identification.

Upon reaching the police station, Insp. Malhotra started the investigation immediately. "Look I am not really in favour of violence nor do I have the energy right now to beat you and get your confession. So, quickly start with your details and then the motive." The man was slightly surprised by the inspector's placid tone and dislike for violence. He thought, "I've nothing else to lose so might as well tell the truth. Might save me from going to hell."

The man started, "My name is Naren Kumble and I stay in the chawls of West Mumbai. I have a 65-year-old father who has Guillain-Barre syndrome and a 55-year-old mother who is going to die next month because of a tumour. My younger sister, Nidhi died 8 years back when she was 9 years old and I was 14. She is actually the main motive behind this murder. I live in a chawl as I mentioned before and my father lost his job because of his syndrome hence the sole breadwinner of the house was my mother. She worked as a maid, cook, and caretaker and sometimes sold various things in the local market like pickles, vegetables, fruits and small knickknacks that my sister and I carved. Despite doing so much she earned only 15 thousand per month which is not a lot if you have a husband who needs thousands worth of medication, two children to educate and feed and a house to run." He then gestured to the inspector for some water as he knew that this conversation would not be a brief one. Aman was curious to hear the rest of the story and told the peon to hurry and get the water. After gulping lots of water Naren resumed with his narration, "When my sister was 8 years old, she got a fever, common cold and dry cough. We thought that it was nothing serious, home remedies and rest would help. But she then started vomiting continuously and her temperature became 103 degrees. We decided to admit her to the nearest government hospital because private ones are out of our league. What we didn't know was that the hospital had a disgusting practice of first taking the full amount of money and then only starting the surgery or treatment. We put her in the emergency department but still, they didn't treat her. My family pleaded with them and my mother even grovelled at their feet. First, they had taken the body inside but then the woman I murdered Kaira Shah flounced out of the room.

After a minute the doctors also came out and said that Kaira hadn't allowed them to do the treatment without getting the money first and that my sister had p-p-passed away

69 – Paulomi Babre

because of untreated brain fever. So, that evil nurse d-d-deserved to die most painfully" Naren stopped speaking and broke down. He was sobbing uncontrollably when the phone rang. Insp. Malhotra answered the phone and a woman cryingly said, "My sister is missing. A note is stuck on my door that she was murdered and taken to the morgue. P-please come f-f-fast and find my s-s-sister." Aman doubted in his mind as he had put a note stating the same at the Shah household and asked, "What did you say your name was and location?" The woman replied, "My name is Kaira Shah." She then said the location which was the place where Naren had killed 'Kaira Shah'! Aman sent a group of constables there. Naren asked, "Who called now?" Aman answered gravely, "The same Kaira Shah you murdered..."

___

Sweet Revenge

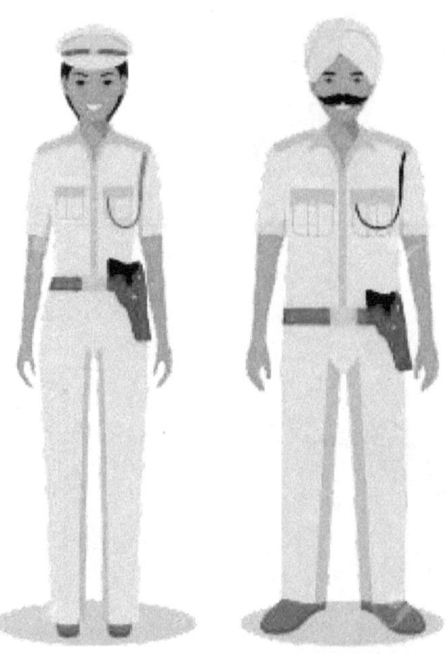

Already on his 3rd cup of strong coffee, SP Sukhwinder (Superintendent Police, not #Sponsered) diligently kept reading through the files. "Ah! These days the crime rate has reduced by a huge margin. No fun only these days. Only files, files and more files," sighed the rather sarcastic SP. His timid ally, Inspector Joshi worriedly said, "Err…Sir, isn't that something to be happy about?"

Sukhwinder guffawed and cheekily replied, "What's life without a few murders here and there?" Joshi let out a mirthless dry chuckle at his senior's dark humour. Well, it was true, from many days there were no homicides or suicides and **almost** all the old cases were solved. As if the dark forces had heard them, the telephone started ringing right on cue. Sukhwinder answered the phone and heard," Sir, PSI Doshi speaking from Thane. One of the constables found a dead body during his daily rounds. Can you come here quickly?" Sukhwinder grimly replied," I will reach you as soon as possible. Keep the general public away not to miss any footprints or handprints. Call the forensic department ASAP." Joshi who had heard the SP had made all arrangements and the pair left for the crime scene immediately. Upon reaching they saw a group of policemen surrounding the forensic department who were crouched near a badly disfigured body. Joshi went over to the policemen to note all the basic details while the SP went ahead towards the body. It was the body of a young barber named Sachin Choudhary and it seemed as though he had been subjected to brutal torture as his stomach was cut open and entrails were badly slashed too. Nearby his wife, mother and father were mourning and lamenting and the constable who had found the body had just come out of the washroom after puking numerous times. The case looked like a plain homicide. Sukhwinder got straight to work and asked the forensic departments for any stray signs. They said that there were few hairs, 2 sets of fingerprints and a stamp on the man's foot. Sukhwinder peered down at his foot and saw a bright blue stamp with the letter R inside a star. Joshi took pictures of the foot, stomach and neck which had red welts on it as though strangled.

It was late at night when all the basic investigations were done and the body was given to the family to perform the rituals. For SP Sukhwinder this case was as though fresh blood had been injected into his body and he felt pumped with energy. He felt as though he had seen the same marks somewhere and removed all the old files. He and Inspector Joshi sat the whole night sifting through the files of pending cases to find some similarities. "Sir, aren't these marks kind of same?" said Joshi pushing the file in front of the weary SP. Sukhwinder pulled the file near and intently gazed at the gruesome picture of a man with his entrails open and his foot had the same mark. Sukhwinder said, "This is a Pune case, right? Call up Inspector Rane and ask him for all the leads they found. Tomorrow morning first thing get the contact list of both Sachin and this guy. We will start shortlisting for similar contact numbers and this mysterious R." Stifling a yawn, Joshi agreed and they finally went home for the night.

The next day morning a rather groggy Inspector Joshi and a super-alert Sukhwinder reached the office at 6 am and started with their inspection. Joshi was slightly ruffled as they had gone home at 2 in the morning and the SP had called him at 5 am as a wake-up call. Sukhwinder went to his superior's office for warrants for the case and the now wide-awake inspector started his work. He reported to Sukhwinder, "Sir, the Pune guy's name is Jay Prakash. And there are 4 common contacts and all four of them are with the letter R- Rahul Jha, Reshma Chatterjee, Raghav Mehta and Radhika Roy." Sukhwinder beamed at the efficient work and started finding out their contact numbers. He said, "While I call these people and grill them, can you check if these 4 or any other contact numbers have ever been on the criminal record?" First Sukhwinder called up Raghav Mehta, who answered on the second ring. "Hello, Dr Raghav Mehta speaking. May I know who are you?" a rather confident voice said. Sukhwinder put on his most baritone voice and replied, "I am Superintendent Sukhwinder from the Mumbai Branch speaking. Do you know Mr Jay Prakash or Mr Sachin Choudhary? "Yes obviously. They both are my childhood friends and we've grown up together. But the untimely death of Jay has saddened me a lot. Why do you ask?" "Well, Mr Sachin was found dead yesterday evening. I may need to meet you later in case the case asks me to but till then take care."

Next up was Ms Reshma Chatterjee but a male voice answered the phone, "Hello, who's this?" Sukhwinder answered, "I am SP Sukhwinder and I want to speak to Ms Reshma." "You fool! How dare you ask an old father to give the phone to his dead daughter. What type of people work in the police force?" Sukhwinder tried to console the angered old man," I am sorry sir. If you don't mind, may I know how she died? Was it a natural death?" The old man now overridden with grief replied, "It's okay beta. My daughter was such an angel, that she has so many well-wishers. She died of lung cancer 3 years back. M-m-my sweet little fairy!" Sukhwinder hastily ended the conversation,

"I didn't mean to upset you, sir. Thank you so much." As SP Sukhwinder went for his 30-minute lunch break, Inspector Joshi dealt with the other two. He first called Mr Rahul Jha. A rather sickly-sounding man answered, "Rahul Jha from Sri Laxmi Laundry speaking. What do you want iron press, dry cleaning, bleaching, dyeing, washing or everything? Nowadays we alter also." Joshi kept the telephone away from his ear as the man was on a rant about the various services. He couldn't take the babble anymore and interrupted sternly, "Hey look I don't want any laundry services. I am Inspector Joshi from the Mumbai branch speaking. What is your relation with Mr Sachin Choudhary and Mr Jay Prakash?" "That buffoon Sachin had his saloon right next to my store and that turd Jay was the owner of a grocery shop on the opposite sidewalk," said the spiteful man. Joshi carefully noted the comments and kept the phone.

Lastly, he called Ms Radhika Roy. A delicate and petite voice answered, "Good morning, this is Radhika Roy from Pets and Co. May I know who's this?" Joshi spoke in a polite tone, "Hello ma'am, this is Inspector Joshi from the Mumbai branch. I just wanted to enquire if you know Mr Sachin Choudhary and Mr Jay Prakash by any chance?" She tittered and said, "Oh! Sachin is one of my oldest friends. Jay was also a close acquaintance and a customer at my shop during the earlier days but I heard that he d-d-died." Joshi noticed that while saying Jay her voice turned cold. He said, "Okay ma'am, I shall get back to you in case I need anything."

As he kept the receiver down, Sukhwinder entered the room and said, "What a tasty lunch that was! Well, Joshi, hope you got some work done, eh?" Inspector Joshi quickly updated him with the investigation regarding the call. "Sir, Rahul Jha is a laundry guy and he hates both of the men. Radhika Roy works or owns Pets and Co, she and Sachin were friends but when she spoke about Jay, her voice was cold." Sukhwinder patted his junior's back and determinedly said, "Take a police jeep and go and visit Dr Raghav's and Reshma Chatterjee's houses and have a word with them and their neighbours about their behaviour. I am going to meet that imbecile Rahul and Radhika, after which I will go and visit Sachin's store." Sukhwinder sped on his bike and reached Jha's dirty laundry. Rahul Jha grumpily came and yelled, "Hey look I don't care who you are but I have a lot of work. Talk fast or get out!" Sukhwinder grabbed the skinny launderer and warned, "Don't try any funny business with me. I am SP Sukhwinder so sit quietly or else I'll clean you the way you wash the clothes. Now sit and tell me why you hate Sachin and Jay." All his grumpiness and confidence oozed out like a pricked balloon, Rahul quietly said, "Sorry sir. So, you see Sachin and Jay were my best friends and we three had decided to start a business together, I had put in the same amount as they had but they gave me only 15% of the shares and once the company did well, they forged my initials and divided the company between them. That's why now I am stuck in this laundry shop and they had enough money that they could dissolve the company and settle right in front of me. Sachin had always wanted to be a hairstylist so he opened his saloon and Jay continued his father's business of grocery. Jay's old mother came and told me that a few months back when he was in Pune with his relatives, he passed away. But she didn't tell me anything else. Yesterday I came back from my village and saw that Sachin's shop had police around it and blood everywhere. What has happened, sir?" Sukhwinder felt that Rahul didn't show any remorse for Jay's death and wasn't surprised by the blood in Sachin's shop and he had the perfect motive. He replied, "None of your business. You better not even peep into the next store otherwise the police are always here to handcuff you."

Sukhwinder then went over to the next shop, Sachin's shop where Insp. Joshi was patiently waiting. Joshi gave a smart salute and then reported, "Raghav and Reshma haven't committed the crime. I have verified with the flight agencies and other sources that Raghav was in London on the day of the murder. He was there two days before the murder and came back only yesterday. On the other hand,

Reshma is really dead, I checked our records and I also found her tombstone. So, both of them are ruled out." Sukhwinder said, "Good job! So, I haven't yet met Radhika but this Rahul guy definitely has something going on. He has the motive and isn't even surprised about the blood in Sachin's shop. When I asked him about Jay, that time also he wasn't sad. Why don't you act like a common man and ask him about his village since he supposedly returned from his village only yesterday? Joshi sped off to do his work while Sukhwinder went to meet the last suspect, Radhika Roy. Joshi wore a simple lungi and shirt and went to Rahul's shop. He stood outside the shop and loudly said, "Aiyo, this new place and that idiot Muthumani put sambar on my clothes. Now what will I do with these dirty clothes in a new place like this?" Jha's greedy ears perked up at the prospect of a new customer from whom he could loot more money as he was new. He went outside and said, "Oh gentleman, I have a laundry shop you come there I will clean the clothes in 30 minutes and give you." Now that the bait had been caught, Mr Venkatesh (aka Insp.

Joshi) went inside and gave the clothes to Jha. Then he started a conversation, "Ai! Come here. Do you know why is police there next door?" Rahul replied, "Some crime must've happened. I came from my village yesterday only." The 'Tamilian gentleman' asked, "Where is your ஊர்? Sorry sorry, your village. How did you go there?" "It is in Ramnagar, the second house next to the Jim Corbett Park. I took a train 2 weeks back and came back also by train. Why do you ask?" Joshi was a bit stumped by the question but then used his wit and said, "Aiyo what to tell you? My tour guide was going to do a North India tour for me but now he has got flu and now I have to plan the trip myself. Hence, I am asking people for places." Thankfully then the clothes were ready and Joshi hastily ran out of the laundry after spending ₹310 on somebody else's clothes.

Meanwhile, allergic Mr Sukhwinder was sitting in Pets and Co where animal fluff was flying everywhere. "A-A-Achoooooooo! Ms Radhika, can you do this fast? If I sit here for 10 minutes more, I will need to be admitted for fits." Radhika who was signing some agreement papers apologetically asked for the last 2 minutes. Distracting himself from the growling dogs and sly cats, he focused on the table and the papers that she was signing. Finally, she completed her work and the demure and tiny woman started talking, "Sorry Mr Sukhwinder, these papers were crucial as today we are shutting down this branch and shifting to Germany. Well, as I said Sachin was a great friend of mine but Jay was not really a close friend. He used to hang out with us but we both never spoke apart from the time he came here to buy a doggie. Rahul Jha, another friend of ours said that Sachin's store has been mobbed by police. Anything serious? I haven't been to his store much as I was in Delhi these days and today morning I returned by flight." Sukhwinder made a mental note to check the flight status for the last few days. "Thanks for taking time out to meet me. I'll make a move."

Joshi had checked Jha's alibi and it was true that he was at his house due to some emergency as confirmed by the Uttarakhand police. Sukhwinder checked the flight details and it was true that this morning a flight from Delhi had reached at noon. They were at a dead end with no suspects or leads. Something was troubling Sukhwinder as he felt as though he was forgetting something. After downing two cups of piping hot chai, he found the answer. He immediately told Joshi to start the jeep and he checked the flight status. Joshi who was used to his boss' instant brainwaves drove speedily to the airport where, as Sukhwinder had predicted, Radhika Roy was sitting on the flight to Germany.

After a hefty struggle for someone so small, Radhika scowled and went to the jail. She then narrated, "Didn't I tell you that we 4 were great friends? Well as Jha might've told you we had started a company where Sachin and Jay cheated us out of it. But that wasn't my main motive. You see years before mine,

Sachin's and Jay's fathers were great friends but the other two cheated him and stole his land. MY FATHER COMMITTED SUICIDE BECAUSE OF THEIR FILTHY FATHERS!" She banged the table in anger and for a minute the officers were quite frightened of the 4'11" woman. She continued, "I grew up without the love of a father. My mother who deeply loved him also died after a few years. I GREW UP AS AN ORPHAN WHILE THEY HAD THE TIME OF THEIR LIVES!! First, I killed Jay by luring his doggie who knew me, outside. Killing Sachin wasn't easy as that fellow was smart but I succeeded in that too. As for my Delhi alibi, it was quite easy. I was indeed in Delhi these days but the day Sachin died I had booked a round trip to Mumbai and by 8 in the morning I was back in my office. So not a soul suspected me, a tiny delicate little darling. Then how did you?" Sukhwinder said, "Remember when I was sitting in your office and you were signing the papers? Well, I was trying to distract myself from the fluff and my eyes settled on your paper. Today when I was later pondering, I realised that the R that you draw while signing for the same R on their foot. It didn't take me much time to go back and find out about your dad which became your motive."

Later as Joshi and Sukhwinder celebrated with some hot tea and oily fritters, Joshi piped up, "Sir congratulations for solving two cases at one time. But sir, I have a small request. Please give me my ₹310 which I spent on that idiot Jha." Both of them burst into peals of laughter and for some time SP Sukhwinder's thirst for murder was quenched.

Who IS Olivia?

It was spring and flowers were blossoming everywhere. Everyone was merrily doing their work and enjoying the pleasant weather. *But amidst all the merry-making and joy, darkness and paranormal activities. Horror was lurking somewhere.*

"Come on, just pull the bag out! Ivy go and help your sister. The cab is not going to wait all day!" yelled an exasperated Iris Baker, their mother. The Bakers had newly arrived in St. Ives. Ivy and Irene were trying to pull their overstuffed suitcase which had been wedged with much difficulty into the backseat. Their enthusiastic calm father, Ian hopped onto the backseat and pushed the bag while his daughters pulled it. After a lot of difficulty, the bag finally toppled out squashing Ivy and Irene. The snappy driver demanded 5 pounds more because he waited for so long and smugly sped away clutching the money. The Bakers turned around and saw the house they had booked. It was a

Victorian-style three-storey house and was quite pretty. But I wish I could say the same about their neighbour's house. It also was a 3-storey house but it had black tinted windows, a lopsided chimney with smoke coming out from it, a greasy door with a broken doorknob and it was painted with green paint which had turned brown over the years. Ivy squealed, "There are children next door! They have a bicycle and a ball outside." Her older sister Irene scolded her, "Shush! Don't talk so loudly, we don't need to wake the whole neighbourhood. Come on in now." Secretly Irene was also pleased with the thought of children to play with. They were weary with all the shifting, thus they sat to eat dinner immediately. Mr Baker gulped hot soup and then said, "Girls, I think you should take some soup and jelly to our new neighbours so that we have good relations with them and maybe then you can play with the kids too." The two sisters happily nodded and their mother agreed to make comforting cabbage soup and Mr Baker would make his famous raspberry caramel jelly.

The next day the girls hopped over to the next-door house and rang the bell. Nobody opened the door for a good 10 minutes but then later a young girl around the age of 10 opened the door. She had strawberry blonde hair and wore a white skirt and T-shirt. She waved and said in a chirpy voice, "Hiya! I'm Olivia. You are?" Ivy and Irene liked her immediately. Ivy replied, "Hi! I am Ivy and this is my 11-year-old sister Irene. I hope we can become friends and play." Irene added, "We've also brought some cold jelly and hot soup for you and your family. By the way, where are your parents?" Olivia replied, "Ooh! I love a good jelly and some hot soup is perfect for my spicy cough. Well, my parents have gone to visit my Gramma. They'll come back next week. Do you guys want to play?" The two sisters nodded and ran back home to get their toys. While going out, their mother said from the kitchen, "If you children mingle well then call her for dinner tomorrow night. Also, ask her if she likes butternut squash soup, strawberry tart and lamb chops with mint sauce." Ivy was excited at the prospect of making a new best friend. The girls have a great time playing and jumping around. Irene asked Olivia, "Hey, will you come home for dinner tomorrow night?" Olivia nodded excitedly as there were no other children in the neighbourhood and it was the first time she had made friends. Ivy piped in, "I hope you like butternut squash soup, lamb chops and strawberry tart because Mum's going to make that for dinner tomorrow." Olivia was slightly stumped at the various dishes but then was happy that after many days she would be able to eat a proper meal.

The next day the Bakers house was a mess. Mr Baker was covered with flour and smelled like strawberries after making the tarts. The whole house had a warm vibe because of the rich squash soup and the mint sauce's smell was just heavenly. Irene was dusting the house while Ivy arranged all the cutlery neatly on the table. Exactly at 7 pm, the bell rang and Olivia stood there in her white costume. As Irene ushered her in, she wondered why their guest always wore the same white clothing. Olivia was greeted very well by the Bakers. Ian cracked silly dad jokes while Iris made her feel welcome. Finally, it was dinner time and it seemed as though Olivia hadn't eaten a good meal in days. She took second helpings of everything and praised the food wholeheartedly. Mrs Baker who was a very kind woman offered to give her food for later too which she promptly agreed.

Ivy and Irene became great friends with Olivia though she was kind of peculiar. They both had similar questions in their minds- "Where were her parents? Why had they left her alone for so many days? Why didn't she change her clothes ever?" Whenever they asked her about her parents, a cold look would come on her face and she would run away. It had been 6 days since the Baker family had shifted but there was no notice of her parents. Iris warned them, "Something seems slightly off about her. Be careful girls. People aren't always what they portray." Ian also said, "I would suggest you play in front of our house only and don't go near her house." The girls were slightly puzzled at their parents' warnings but obeyed them. The next day Ivy who was very curious asked Olivia out of the blue while they were swaying on the swings, "Why don't you ever wear something else apart from this white garb?" Olivia gave her a cold stare, pushed her swing roughly and ran to her house. Irene caught her sister's hand in time otherwise she would've toppled off the swing. Ivy was very hurt at her new best friend's behaviour but at the same time, she was inquisitive.

For the next 3 days, Olivia didn't come to play. The sisters ignored it as they were upset with her for her bad comportment. But on the fourth day, they were worried as she didn't even come out to collect the milk bottles that were piling up outside her house. They expressed their concern to their parents but they said, "It's okay. She must be ashamed of her behaviour. Maybe that's why she isn't coming out. But if she doesn't come out for more days then, we'll come with you to her house." That night at around midnight or later, a car drove into the next-door driveway. The Bakers decided to go and meet Olivia's parents the next day.

The next morning the Bakers warily went over to the Morgan household. They climbed up the slippery steps and Ian stepped forward and rang the bell. After 5 minutes a red-haired couple opened the door. Ivy said, "Hello, we are the Bakers. Well, since the past few days, your daughter Olivia has become our great friend." Irene continued, "But for 5 days she isn't coming to play. Can you please inform her that we asked for her?"

The couple exchanged a frightened and confused look. Then Olivia's mother said, "Umm… girls, which daughter?" Her father added, "Our daughter Olivia has been dead for the past 4 years because of the spicy cough."

____

95 – Paulomi Babre

Lost Love

"I know you crossed a road that I can't
follow

Since your love is all, I have
I want you to know

If I can't be close to you
I'll settle for the spirit of you"

"Seriously?! Why does the same music keep playing after every fortnight?!" yelled Tara, a 5-year-old naughty girl. Her parents, Akshay and Shruti were police officers. As Tara mentioned every fortnight the music used to be sung. Akshay remarked, "I've been keeping a note of the lyrics. I have figured out now that it's sung by a poet or a philosopher to his lost love.' Shruti added, "Also have you noticed that he sings the song on every full moon night?" The three of them just shrugged it aside because who cares about an old poet? After a couple of days, the incident was forgotten until at the police station a case came up. A particular choir girl called Laila had died 2 years back but nobody had solved the case. She had died due to murder. Akshay was puzzled, "Why hadn't anybody taken action on the case then? Was there some political handling here?" Shruti was also thinking along the same lines, "After sooo many years, why did the case open up now?" The pair opened the case's file and found that the girl's parents had lodged many complaints but nobody had bothered to solve the case. The case was highly mysterious from every angle. They decided to pay a visit to the girl's parents so that they could find out more about the case. Just as they were about to leave the police station, a constable came running and said, "Sir there is another case closely related to the Laila one. Exactly 14 days before a man called Manoranjan passed away. It states that he drank poison and died."

Shruti and Akshay noted it and went to Laila's house. There an elderly man opened the door and welcomed them inside. His wife was also sitting listlessly on a chair. The old man noticed the couple's glances at his wife and said, "After the day our daughter died, her mental health collapsed." Akshay asked politely, "If you don't mind may I ask something? Do you have any idea who might've killed her? Any enemies or trouble-makers?" Laila's father warily looked around and then whispered, "Laila was in love with a stupid poet called Manoranjan. I simply refused to let her marry him because he always seemed kind of shady to me and also, I didn't want her to depend on a man who barely had a roof on his head. So, I think that he might've killed her." Shruti said, "But in one of our old files it is mentioned that he died 14 days before her death. Either someone has tampered with the file or something suspicious is going on." After thanking her parents, the pair went back to the station. The next day as they sat brooding on the case, Laila's father came to the station. He said, "I need to confess something. Manoranjan had told me that at any cost he would have Laila. I was worried for my daughter's life so I sent a few goons to threaten him. But when they reached, he had already drunk the poison." Akshay said, "Sir, please don't hide anything else further on. Every bit is crucial for the case." Her father hung his head in shame and then went out. That night at home their daughter Tara said, "Daddy, that song will probably play today because today is a full moon." At first, Akshay chuckled then it dawned to him, "Shruti!! The song that is sung every night is by Manoranjan's spirit to Laila!" Shruti worked out the facts and everything led to that reasoning. The next day at work, they thought, "Probably Laila must've killed herself on a pretence of murder so that she could be reunited with the love of her life." Just as they thought of this possibility, a constable came running and said, "Sir, those files were tampered with. Manoranjan died 14 days after Laila by suicide. And it was again a full moon..."

Answers to a few of your Questions

- ✓ **What is the mystery after Officer Ethan's statement at the end of "The Bloody Prom"?**

Ans: Liam Blaise was the gangster Antonio's son! When the lights had gone out for the first time, Antonio's men had taken Chloe to a corner the way it was shown in the CCTV camera. When Liam had gone to 'search' for Chloe, the lights had gone out the second time and gave him enough time to write the message with paint. Since some paint had fallen on him, he didn't dare to go back to the prom. Liam had once come to Chloe's house to give some Easter eggs and when he was leaving, he heard, "I think that our information on Antonio should be sufficient for the police to track. Let's polish it a bit more and attach more proof and facts so that it will be a satisfactory piece." As a good son, Liam couldn't bear his father being found or worse killed, so he decided to kill both of them to avoid any leaks of the info. When Chloe regained consciousness and saw Liam coming to kill her, all the pieces of the puzzle fit in her head but before she could tell anybody about it, she was dead. Liam had used her blood to write the message Liam knew that he would be the last one to be suspected because he was Chloe's boyfriend after all who was 'distraught' after her disappearance. But he had made the folly of giving his blazer to the launderers and thus, his plan unravelled. Ah! Won't every father want such an adoring son?

✓ **If Naren murdered Kaira Shah, then who had called the police station with the same address and the same name?**

Ans: Well, if you are thinking it's paranormal activities, you are wrong! Kaira and Kashvi Shah were two twins. Kaira was the nurse but she hadn't told the doctors not to perform the surgery. On the other hand, she had told them to do the surgery first and the bills could be paid off later. But to save their name, after she flounced out, they used her name and put off the surgery. When Naren went to the Shah household, Kashvi had come from work and was resting. But Naren didn't know that the woman was not the one he had to kill. But since he didn't know that they were twins he killed Kashvi. Later when Kaira had come home and found her sister dead, she had phoned the police station. Alas! Kashvi died in vain but so did Naren's sister...

✓ **If Olivia was dead then who was the girl talking to the sisters?**

Ans: Olivia Morgan was an 8-year-old when she passed away so she had some wishes as a child. She wanted to enjoy some more time as a kid. It is said that many a time spirits stay back to fulfil some things that aren't unfulfilled. So, Olivia had fun with the girls, but once she understood that the girls were gaining on her secret, she decided to vanish again. Spicy cough killed her but nothing could kill her childish spirit and her wish to live more.

✓ **If Manoranjan died after Laila, then who killed her? And why does the full moon keep interfering everywhere?**

Ans: Manoranjan had faked his death the day the goons had come so that he wouldn't be thrashed to death. The next day he got news that Laila's father was arranging her marriage with another guy. He loved her so much that he would rather kill her than see her live with another person who was not him. So, on the full moon, he got a little crazy and on the pretence of meeting her for the last time, he murdered her ruthlessly. The next day he realised his folly and came to know that with her dead he couldn't live anymore. On the next full moon, he killed himself. Oh! Their love story ended up quite gruesome, didn't it?

Congratulations, fellow adventurer! As you close this book, remember: that every ending is just a new beginning. Carry the lessons learned, the characters cherished, and the adventures embarked upon, into your own story. I hope the words within these pages have resonated with you and brought value to your life. Let imagination be your compass, and curiosity your guide. Remember, stories have the power to inspire, comfort, and transform us. For in the realm of books, the journey never truly ends. What tale will you embark upon next?